Foxy DuBois and Alphonso Alligator

in:

The Cunning Plan

Introducing
Foxy DuBois

She's smart. She's cute.

And she'll do anything
to get rid of Alphonso.

and
Alphonso the Alligator

He's mean.
He's hungry.
And if Foxy doesn't
feed him he's going
to eat HER!

and Tony Ravioli

He's... err... he's the barman.

and Special Guest:

Mr Billy Bongo
as
Little Norman

Yep, he's cute.

DISCLAIMER:

No animals were humiliated, teased or eaten in the production of this book.

WARNING:

Contains copious amounts of alligator slobber and scenes of small animals dressed in fluffy clothing, which some readers may find distressing.

*O*nce upon a time, there was a happy little fox. She lived in a huge posh house with fancy wallpaper and chandeliers and proper family portraits on the wall. She spent her days eating sugared almonds and having tantrums when she didn't get her own way. She had the sort of childhood that you and I could only dream about.

And when she grew up, Foxy DuBois spent her time buying shoes and going to flashy parties

and having
even bigger tantrums
when she didn't get her
own way, even though she was
far too old to be throwing herself
on the floor and kicking her skinny
little legs.

But then one day, her life changed. And
not for the better. Because on that day,
she met Alphonso!

Do you remember being born? Well
no. Of course you don't. But you
know that you were born, right?
Well Alphonso Alligator was
not born. Oh no.

He hatched.
From an EGG! And
when he arrived in the
world he had nobody to love
him or buy him cute little jumpers
with rabbits on. In fact, the first
person Alphonso saw was Foxy
DuBois and she didn't want to chub
his cheeky chops or bounce him up and
down on her knee. No. She wanted to
EAT him!

Luckily for Alphonso, Foxy's plan
to get rid of him well and truly
backfired, because as it turned
out, Alphonso was big. And
mean. And had very, very
sharp teeth!

Welcome to Vaudeville

As you can see, we're not in the smartest part of town. And I hope you're wrapped up warm, because it's very chilly out there this morning.

If you squint your eyes, you might

just make out the shape of a small chicken, hurrying down the dimly-lit street.

She scuttles between the run down low-rise apartment blocks that she calls home, pulling her scarf tightly around her skinny neck to keep out the cold.

Suddenly, you hear a scuffle from an upstairs window. And was that a scream? Later the chicken will tell her friend, uncertainly, that it was probably a cat. But you and I both know it was no cat. For in a shabby, third-floor apartment on this very street, Alphonso the Alligator is up to

Chapter 1

In Which Foxy DuBois Plans to Get Rich Quick

'**G**et me six roasted chickens with NO salad and a double fudge sundae with a pink umbrella or the FOX GETS IT!'

An enormous alligator burst through the door of the East Street Eazy Diner, dangling a startled-looking fox by the ankle.

The fox struggled like a wildcat.
She shoved a hair curler up the
alligator's gigantic scaly nostril
and yanked his waxed moustache
in an attempt to free herself.

'Get your filthy claws off
me you blubber-brained
brute!' she yelled. 'I'm
not even dressed!'

You see, this was no
ordinary fox. Oh no. This
was Miss Foxy DuBois
and she was NOT happy.

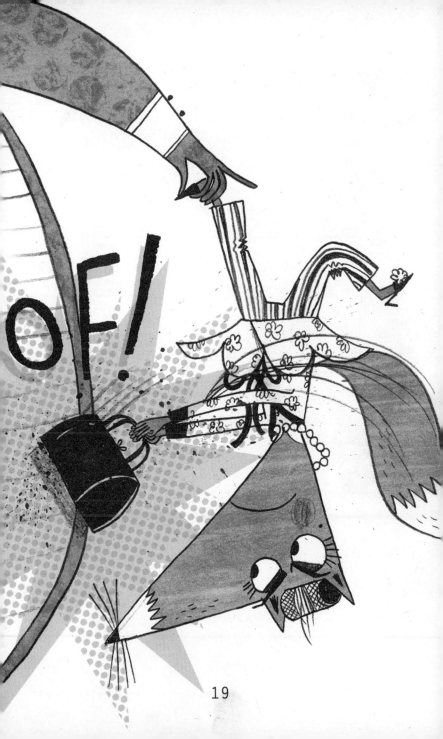

OF!

19

The barman, one Tony Ravioli, dived into the kitchen. 'OK, Alphonso,' he called. 'Take it easy Big Guy. Your breakfast's on its way.'

Alphonso dropped the fox on her head and squeezed his enormous belly in behind the table, slobbering hungrily.

Foxy picked herself up, straightened her curlers and smiled wryly at the terrified onlookers.

'He's a nice alligator, really,' she grimaced. Then she slumped in a chair and put her head in her paws.

'Of all the doorsteps in all the world, why did you have to turn up on mine?' she groaned to Alphonso. 'I had a lovely house, and plenty of money. I had SHOES! Now it's all gone, thanks to you.'

Poor Foxy. Since meeting Alphonso she had been a little down on her luck. In fact, she had been a whole lot down on her luck.

If luck were an elevator, Foxy DuBois would be seventeen floors below the basement.

That's how down she was. That irritating alligator had eaten her out of house and home, and now every day was a struggle to keep him fed. If she didn't, he would happily swallow her whole, and still have room for cake.

But food cost money, and Foxy didn't have a bean. She pulled a notepad out of her bag, and tried to think of a plan.

THINGS IN FOXY'S HANDBAG:

ALLIGATOR REPELLENT (DOESN'T WORK)

PURSE (EMPTY!)

ALPHONSO'S BELLY BUTTON FLUFF. (YUCK!)

PEN (NIBBLED BY ALPHONSO)

NOTEPAD

HOW TO MAKE MONEY FAST

~~a. Rob a bank~~

(Too risky)

~~b. Marry someone rich~~

(Ewww)

~~c. Win the lottery~~

(No money to buy a ticket)

~~d. Kidnap someone important~~

(Against the law)

e. Get a job

NIBBLED BY ALPHONSO

Suddenly, Alphonso's eyes lit up.
'Food!' he grinned, making a grab
for the piled-high plates Tony was
carrying. But Tony held them just
out of reach. 'That'll be ten bucks,'
he said.

Cool as a cucumber, Foxy DuBois
tore a page from her notebook.
She scribbled something on it and
handed the note to the barman.

'Tony, darling,' she said,
smoothly. 'I'm a little short of
cash at the moment. You
know how it is. Here's an
I Owe You.'

'Aww, Foxy, Foxy, Foxy,' sighed Tony, 'I'd love to help you out, really I would. But I have enough IOUs here to paper the walls of the Empire State Building. If you're short of cash, you'll just have to earn some. There's a mountain of dirty dishes out the back that need a good scrub if you want a job.'

Foxy bristled. 'I am a lady!' she said haughtily. 'I do NOT wash up!'

'Ah well.' Tony shook his head and turned back to the kitchen with the plates.

Alphonso glared hungrily at Foxy and licked his lips.

'WAIT!' she cried, thinking quickly. 'I meant to say, I can't do your washing up, because... because... I already have a job. Look!' She grabbed a newspaper, turned to the Situations Vacant page and read out the first job advert she saw.

WANTED
RELIABLE DOG WALKER
FOR SIX DELIGHTFUL LAPDOGS
Excellent rate of pay.
Would suit retired person.
Madame V. Fowl,
1003 Rooster Way
note: predators need not apply
BREAKS FOR LESS
FREE 2ND WEEK
Aupair needed
call 0088 4587 99
NOW!

'You see? Come on, Tony darling,' she pleaded. 'Just give us the nosh, and I'll pay for it later, I promise!'

But Tony was not to be fooled. 'You get the job first. Then old grouchy chops can eat as many ice cream sundaes as he likes.' And he chased the naughty pair out of the café and locked the door.

Chapter 2

In Which Alphonso Puts on a Dress and Lipstick

Alphonso was livid. 'I want my breakfast!' he growled. 'And if I don't get my breakfast I'm going to eat YOU!'

But Foxy stood her ground. That job advert had given her an idea.

An idea so brilliant that in no time at all she would be living it up in that swanky beach house she had always dreamed of – sipping iced lemonade and eating chocolate with not an alligator in sight. All she had to do was trick Alphonso into helping her, and then make her escape!

'Well, I suppose you *could* eat me,' she said, slyly, 'but then you'll never get the chance to try the all-you-can-eat buffet at the Grand Hotel.'

Alphonso's eyes widened and
he grabbed Foxy. 'An all-you-
can-eat buffet!'
he gasped.

'I'd do
anything...
anything for just
a sniff of an all-
you-can-eat
buffet.'

Foxy peeled Alphonso's sharp claws off her skinny arms and looked into his yellow eyes. 'That's settled then,' she said. 'But you must do exactly what I say.'

FEED THE ALLIGATOR

AND GET RICH PLAN:

- Alphonso dresses as dog walker

- Alphonso keeps Madame Fowl talking, by offering dog walking service

- Clever Foxy secretly steals the dogs

- Alphonso pretends to find the dogs

- Grateful old lady gives Alphonso large reward 💲💲💲💲💲

- Foxy + Alphonso = RICH

Back at their apartment,
Foxy DuBois explained her plan.

Alphonso was not convinced.
'It's a stupid plan,' he said.
'Madame Fowl will never ask
me to find her dogs. I'm the
meanest predator in town.'

Foxy grabbed Alphonso and
pulled him close. 'You may be
the meanest,' she hissed, 'but
I'm the smartest. Now come
on. We've got work to do.'

Foxy rummaged through a box of old clothes and picked out a flowery dress, a woolly shawl, a pair of glasses, a fancy hat with a feather on the top and a pair of ridiculous high-heeled shoes. She thrust them at Alphonso.

'I'm not wearing those!' gasped Alphonso. 'They're SO last year!'

'Just hurry up and get dressed,' snapped Foxy.

She applied some lipstick to

Alphonso's scaly mouth and pulled a pair of white gloves over his claws. 'There,' she smiled. 'You look just like my Aunt Evie – a lovely, sweet old lady who loves dogs.

Now try to behave and whatever you do, don't open your mouth too wide. We won't get within a mile of those precious pooches if Madame Fowl sees all those teeth.'

The two rogues left the apartment, and set off.

If you'd been in the park that morning, playing with the other kids on the swings, you would have seen a smart-looking fox walking with her elderly friend.

You would have stopped to stare as the old lady grabbed a passing chicken only to be rugby-tackled to the ground by the fox, who proceeded to sit on her friend's head while the chicken fled through the park, squawking in alarm.

And if you'd had any sense at all,
you would have jumped off your
swing and run away, as fast as
your skinny legs could carry you.

Chapter 3

In Which Foxy Takes Someone Else's Dogs For a Walk

1003 Rooster Way was a magnificent mansion. It stood at the end of a sweeping gravel drive and was surrounded by a neatly-clipped hedge.

'You keep the old lady talking,' hissed Foxy, 'and I'll do the rest. Meet me by the park fountain in one hour.' Then she slipped round the back of the house and through a hole in the hedge.

Alphonso crunched nervously up the gravel drive. He was about to knock on the gleaming front door when he spotted something small and brown, scurrying across the grass. Quick as a flash, the gluttonous alligator grabbed the fluffy little creature. He was about to toss it into his gaping jaws when he was interrupted by a sharp voice.

'You, there!'

Alphonso-dressed-as-Aunt-Evie

jumped so hard his bloomers
fell down. He whipped the tasty
morsel behind his back and tried
to look innocent.

'What are you doing in
my garden?' It was
Madame Fowl.
She was leaning
out of an upstairs
window, her
face half hidden
by a huge pair
of thick-rimmed
glasses.

MADAME FOWL

52

'Oh, good day to you,' squeaked
Alphonso, nervously. 'I'm a – a
kindly old lady who loves eating –
err, I mean, *walking* dogs.'
He pulled the poor, terrified
animal out from behind his back
and clumsily stroked the cowering
chihuahua. 'I've come about
the job,' he added.

The front door creaked open
and a wizened old man beckoned
him in. 'Vipe your feet,' he
growled, 'Madame will be down
in a moment.' Then he eased the

shivering little dog out of
Alphonso's tightly clenched
fist, and placed it gently on the
ground. The chihuahua lifted
his leg against Alphonso's ankle,
barked defiantly, and trotted
into the house.

Alphonso shook his wet leg in disgust. 'I should have eaten that pesky fox when I had the chance,' he grumbled, bitterly. 'At least then I'd have a full belly.'

Instead he was standing in a horrid puddle, dressed in a hideously unfashionable outfit, pretending to be nice. This was most definitely NOT a good day.

Just then, Madame Fowl glided down the grand staircase towards him.

She peered closely at her visitor through lenses so thick they made her eyes bulge. 'You're not a predator are you?' she hissed, studying his smudged lipstick suspiciously. 'Only, I don't LIKE predators.'

'Oh, no, no, no, no, no!' squeaked Alphonso. 'Although I did look a bit of a fright this morning – it's my skin, you see. I just can't seem to find the right moisturiser.' He rearranged his shawl and held out a gloved claw. 'I'm Aunt Evie, dear.

Pleased to meet you.'

Madame Fowl looked 'Aunt Evie'
up and down. 'Well, Tiddles did
seem to like you,' she snapped.

She turned to her butler. 'Max,
bring the dogs. All of them –
Tiddles and Pickles and Pansy
and Fluffy and Muffin and Little
Norman. There's someone
I'd like them to meet.'

Max shuffled off, but soon
reappeared looking very agitated.

'Madame,' he stuttered. 'Ze dogs are not zere. Zey have been stolen!'

'STOLEN?!' shrieked Madame Fowl. 'What do you mean, they've been stolen?' Max backed away nervously. 'D-don't vorry, Madame,' he stammered. 'I'll find zem.'

'You?' snorted Madame Fowl. 'You couldn't find an elephant in a mouse cage!' Then she clutched

Alphonso's gloved claw. 'Aunt Evie,' she pleaded. 'You have to help me. Please find my babies before something happens to them!'

Chapter 4

In Which Foxy's Get Rich Plan Begins to Unravel

As you have probably worked out already, Alphonso was not the brightest of creatures. Most of his brain had been used up by now, what with the dressing up, and the small talk, and the effort it took to balance in those ridiculous shoes.

As a result, he had completely
forgotten Foxy's plan!

He had forgotten that it was
Foxy who'd kidnapped
the dogs.

He. Was. Furious!

How was he going to get enough
dog-walking money for his all-you-
can-eat buffet if there were no dogs
to walk? And where was that oh-so-
clever fox? Wasn't she supposed to
be helping?

'Don't worry, Madame Fowl,' he
snarled. 'I have an excellent sense
of smell. I'll find your Tiddles, and
Toddles and Piddles and... and
Widdles, if it's the last thing I do.'

Foxy, meanwhile, was on her way to the park, carrying six rather puzzled dogs.

Her plan had worked perfectly. While Madame Fowl was talking to kind old 'Aunt Evie', Foxy had crept in through an open back window and kidnapped all six of Madame Fowl's dogs.

'I am simply awesome!' she chuckled to herself. 'Now all we need to do is put our feet up for an hour, then return the dogs and collect our reward!

Then I'll take Alphonso to the Grand Hotel for his nosh-up. While he's busy stuffing his face, I'll jump on the first train out of this dismal city and get away to the fine life I deserve!'

Safely in the park with the dogs, Foxy sat down to eat a large cream

donut that she had found
in Madame Fowl's kitchen.

Suddenly she was grabbed by
the neck and shaken so hard her
teeth rattled.

'Somebody has stolen the dogs!'
snarled Alphonso. 'And I bet you
had something to do with
it, you... you... sneaky little...
err... FOX!'

'Gaaaaaahhh!' gasped Foxy.
'Tell me where they are or I'll eat
you!' growled the alligator. Foxy
pointed frantically towards the
dogs. 'Thhhhhhhh!' she wheezed.

Tiddles and Pickles and Pansy
and Fluffy and Muffin and
Little Norman were cowering
underneath the bench,
shivering with fright.
'Ah-ha!' snarled Alphonso.
'There they are! Thought you
could hide them did you?' He
lifted Foxy high above his head
and opened his mouth wide.

'Wait!' pleaded Foxy. 'Don't you
remember our plan?'

Alphonso looked blank.

Suddenly Foxy remembered the donut. 'Don't eat me!' she shouted. 'Eat this!' She waved the half-eaten cake in Alphonso's face then flung it into the pond.

Alphonso looked from Foxy, to the dogs, to the donut. Then he dropped Foxy on her head and dived in after the cake.

But a tiny flash of brown fur had streaked ahead of him and clamped the donut in its jaws. Little Norman had taken one look at the delicious

cream cake and decided it
was his. He was now streaking
joyfully across the park with
his prize.

As the other dogs gave chase,
Alphonso managed to grab
hold of their pink leads. He
wasn't going to let these pesky
dogs get away!

Chapter 5

In Which Alphonso's Appetite Gets the Better of Him

When, at last, Foxy came around, her head was throbbing. She sat up dizzily and blinked hard. 'Alphonso?' she croaked. But Alphonso, and all six of Madame Fowl's dogs, were gone.

'ALPHONSOOOO!'

But Alphonso didn't answer. He didn't answer, because he didn't hear Foxy calling. And he didn't hear Foxy calling because he was fast asleep. His enormous, full belly rose and fell gently as he lay, snoring, beneath a tree.

His jaws were smeared red, and he was dreaming happily.

'Mmmm, I love dogs... delicious... in a bun...' he muttered. By his side were six pink leads. And attached to the leads were six little pink coats, containing... nothing! Tiddles and Pickles and Pansy and Fluffy and Muffin and Little Norman were nowhere to be seen.

When at last she found him,
Foxy DuBois stood over the
snoring monster and put
her head in her hands.

'Oh no,' she whispered, despair
creeping over her. 'Tell me you
haven't eaten Madame Fowl's
dogs!'

Dreamily, Alphonso muttered,
'… Eaten dogs.'

'Arrrgggghhhh!'

Alphonso heard a distant groan as he dreamed. Surely his belly wasn't rumbling again?

Suddenly, Alphonso felt a heavy weight flump down on his stomach. He opened a sleepy eye to find Foxy DuBois, sitting right on top of his enormous belly, her head in her hands. 'Oh Alphonso,' she muttered, 'what have you done?'

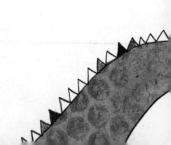

Alphonso sat up, drowsily, toppling Foxy into a tangled heap beside him. He rubbed his eyes. 'Err... I ... Sorry,' he slurred. 'Was I snoring?'

Foxy groaned. 'Yes, you were snoring but — !'

'Well, why didn't you wake me up?' yawned Alphonso. 'You usually wake me up when I snore.'

'But I just — aaarrgh! Never mind.'

'Never mind about the snoring?' said Alphonso. 'But you HATE it when I snore, you're always telling me how annoying it is and now you say it doesn't matter? How's an alligator supposed to — ?'

Foxy jumped to her feet in frustration. 'Just FORGET about the snoring for one second and LISTEN!' she yelled.

'OK! Keep your wig on!' grumped Alphonso.

Foxy took a deep breath.
'Alphonso,' she said carefully.
'You've eaten Madame's dogs,
haven't you? That's why you've
got red stuff smeared around
your face and a big full belly. You
ate Tiddles and Pickles and Pansy
and Fluffy and Muffin and Little
Norman and then you fell asleep.
You've eaten the dogs and now
my plan is RUINED!'

She sat back down in despair.
'What am I going to DO?'
she sobbed.

Alphonso had had enough.
'I haven't eaten anyone's dogs!'
he growled.

'You haven't?'

'No. I haven't.'

'Well, why were you smacking
your lips and muttering about
eating dogs in a bun?' said Foxy.

'I was muttering about eating
dogs, because I like eating dogs.
HOT dogs. You know, the kind

you get from the HOT DOG MAN,
covered in red tomato ketchup
and nestled in a delicious bun?' He
pointed towards a ransacked burger
van. 'An alligator's got to eat.'

Foxy grabbed the empty dog leads and waved them in Alphonso's face. 'And the dogs are...?' she asked.

Alphonso looked around and shrugged. 'They must have wandered off,' he said.

'Wandered off?' gasped Foxy. 'WANDERED OFF! How are we EVER going to find them? This park is HUGE!'

Alphonso blinked lazily and wiped tomato sauce off his chin with his woolly shawl. 'Why don't you just give up?' he yawned.

But Foxy was absolutely not about to give up. Those dogs and the reward money were her ticket out of that miserable town and away from Alphonso. She had to find them, and quickly. But the park was vast. There was no way she could do this on her own.

Chapter 6

In Which Foxy and Alphonso Set Off in Search of Six Runaway Dogs

'You're right,' said Foxy slyly. 'Perhaps we should give up looking. After all, Madame Fowl doesn't even know I exist, so she's hardly likely to suspect *me* of stealing her precious pets. On the other hand, she might wonder why sweet Aunt Evie never came back...'

A worried look crept across Alphonso's face.

'I hear they do a very nice menu
of bread and water in jail,' Foxy
added, innocently.

And so the pair took the leads and empty doggy coats and set off in search of six pampered pooches. They looked behind trees...

And in bushes...

They looked under things...

And down holes...

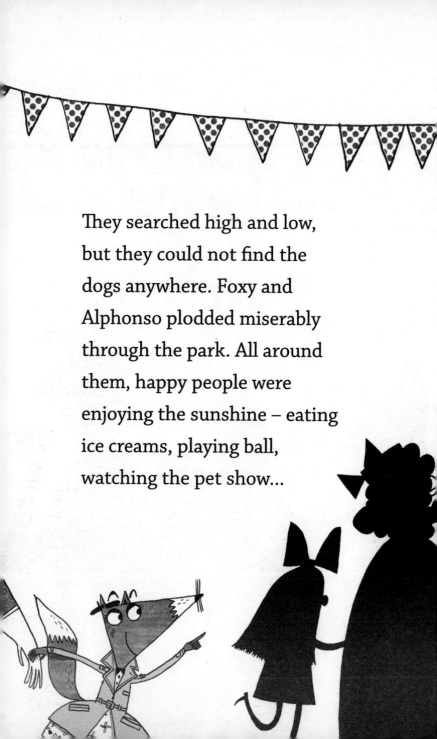

They searched high and low, but they could not find the dogs anywhere. Foxy and Alphonso plodded miserably through the park. All around them, happy people were enjoying the sunshine – eating ice creams, playing ball, watching the pet show...

Foxy's whiskers began to twitch.
A sly smile spread across her
foxy face.

Alphonso, too, was staring at the
assortment of boxes, crates and
tanks being heaved onto
the tables.

'Are you thinking what I'm
thinking?' smiled Foxy.

Alphonso nodded, licking his lips.
'Snack time!' he grinned.

'No!' cried Foxy. 'That's not the all-you-can-eat-buffet, you loony! It's the perfect place to find some pretty pooches to replace the ones you lost! All you have to do is pretend to be the judge, then steal the six dogs that look most like Madame Fowl's.'

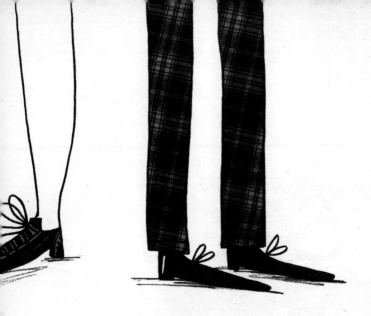

Quiet as a stoat in slippers,
Foxy crept into the tea tent
and tied the real judge's
shoelaces together.

Then she whipped a white
coat from a peg, stuffed
Alphonso into it and shoved
the alligator into the arena.

Then she hid behind
the tent to watch.

Cats hissed and dug in their claws.
Budgies flapped frantically in their
cages. Rats scuttled under their
straw. And their young owners
stared, wide-eyed, as Alphonso-
the-judge stalked around the
tables, peering at the petrified pets.

He lifted a tiny, grey kitten by
the scruff of its neck and gave it
a good sniff.

'A-are you going to eat
my kitty?' whimpered
the cat's owner.

'Chill out, kid,' drawled Alphonso.
'I'm not that desperate.'

'HELP!' shrieked a voice.

'What's going on?' It was
the real judge! She hobbled out of
the tea tent, tripped over
her laces and fell
flat on her
face in the
mud.

'Uh oh!' thought Alphonso,
and quick as a flash he grabbed
an armful of animals and made
a run for it.

Foxy was hot on his heels as
they fled up the hill, before
plunging, panting and puffing,
into some thick bushes.

Chapter 7

In Which Alphonso Presents Foxy With a Tortoise

'I think we got away with it,' puffed Foxy, peeping through the leaves. 'Now hurry up and get those pets into these doggy coats. Then we can give them to Madame Fowl, collect our reward and go home.'

She rummaged inside Alphonso's
bulging coat, and pulled out...

'... A TORTOISE??!!!'

Foxy gaped at the brown, scaly
creature in her hands. The tortoise
pulled its old man's head and little
stubbly legs back into its shell,
and scowled at his captors.

'Oh GREAT!' Foxy sighed. 'This is
ALL I need.'

'Glad to be of service,' grinned Alphonso. He opened his coat to reveal the other animals he'd snatched:

a rabbit

a duck

a hamster

a Siamese cat

and a

fat brown goat.

Foxy DuBois shook her head in despair. 'You bubble-brained bumpkin!' she groaned. 'You don't honestly expect Madame to believe these are her delightful dogs? She might be short-sighted, but she's not blind!'

But there was no time to argue. Thundering across the park towards them came one angry judge, two irate park keepers and a whole crowd of cross pet owners.

There they are!' shouted the judge. 'Get them!'

Quick as a flash, Foxy and Alphonso stuffed the animals into the doggy coats and clipped on the leads. They ran, half dragging, half carrying the stolen pets...

through the trees...

up and down the skate ramps...

around the maze...

 across the lake...

in and out of the marching band...

through the train tunnel...

and out through the park gates.

125

Chapter 8

In Which Foxy is Well and Truly Rumbled

'My darlings! You're home!' Madame Fowl rushed into the hallway and scooped up the tortoise-dog, hugging it close.

'There, there,' she gushed. 'My poor Little Norman, you do look ill.

Did the nasty robber give you
a fright?'

She felt on top of her head for
her glasses so she could get a
closer look, but they weren't
there. And they weren't there
because a certain, scheming Fox
had plucked them off and tucked
them safely away in her pocket.

'Allow me to introduce myself,'
said Foxy, smoothly. 'I'm Funella
Flostrop. Aunt Evie here called
me as soon as she heard your

beautiful – err – babies had gone missing. I helped her to find them.'

Madame Fowl called to her butler. 'Max! Max!' she cried. 'Bring that large bundle of notes from the safe! Miss Flostrop and Aunt Evie have saved my dogs. They must have a reward!'

Then, addressing the tortoise-dog, the old lady crooned, 'Now then, Little Norman, give Miss Flostrop and Aunt Evie a big kissy kiss for rescuing you.'

She thrust the tortoise towards Alphonso's snout, expecting the 'dog' to give his saviour a slimy wet lick.

But the tortoise had other ideas. He was fed up with being dragged around, and Little Norman's pink coat was making him hot.

So when the alligator's gigantic warty nose appeared in front of him, the tortoise did the only thing a tortoise can do in these situations. He opened his tough little beak and BIT. Hard.

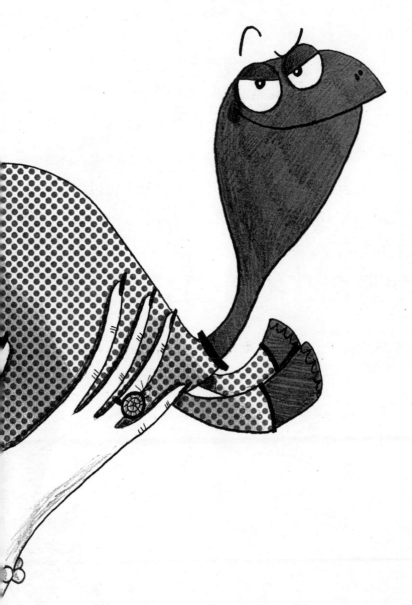

CHOMP!

'ARRRGGGGHHHH!!!!'

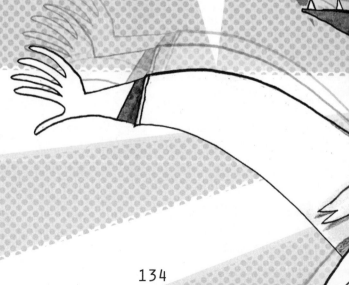

Alphonso-dressed-as-Aunt-Evie leapt in the air, with the determined tortoise attached firmly to his nose. A horrified Madame Fowl tried to pull 'Little Norman' off, but the only things that came off were Alphonso's disguise and Little Norman's coat.

'EEEEEKKKKKK!' screamed Madame Fowl. 'A PREDATOR!' She waved 'Aunt Evie's' glasses and hat in the air. 'And THAT'S not Little Norman! It's a horrible scaly REPTILE!'

She grabbed a feather duster and started jabbing at Alphonso's huge belly. 'What have you done with Little Norman, you big bully?'

Just as Max arrived clutching hundreds of bank notes, the front door burst open. In swarmed the angry judge, the two park keepers and the crowd of cross pet owners.

'MY RABBIT!' cried a small girl.

'MY GOAT!' cried a boy.

'GRAB THEM!' screamed the park keeper. He made a dive for the kidnapped cat, but skidded on the slippery floor and slid headlong

into Madame Fowl's priceless
egg-cup collection.

'MY EGG CUPS!' screeched
Madame Fowl.

'My lovely clean floor...'
sobbed Max.

Foxy DuBois regarded the chaos
and sighed. How could such a
simple plan go so totally and
utterly wrong? There was no hope
of getting even a tiny reward now.

All her hard work had come to
nothing. Or had it?

And with that thought, Foxy tiptoed quietly out of the hallway and slipped through the back door, leaving Alphonso to take all the blame. 'With any luck the police will grab him, lock him up and throw away the key,' she thought. 'And I will be free!'

But even that was not to be, because the ground began to shake and a great rumble filled the air...

People and animals spilled out of the house, coughing and choking and gasping for air. You see, even a very large, very greedy alligator cannot eat a whole burger van load of hot dogs without getting just a little gas.

BBBRRRRRRRAAAAAl

His tummy relieved, Alphonso saw Foxy escaping and shot across the garden with remarkable speed. 'COME BACK HERE, YOU DOUBLE-CROSSING, BUSHY-TAILED PIECE OF FUR!' he yelled.

Foxy dived into the garden shed, jumped on the lawnmower and sped off across the grass. Not to be outdone, Alphonso grabbed the nearest thing on wheels and gave chase.

Chapter 9

In Which Alphonso Gets a Slap-Up Meal and Foxy Gets Her Just Desserts

'Quick, Tony!' shouted Foxy, jumping off her lawnmower. 'Hide me!' She rushed through the door of Tony Ravioli's East Street Eazy Diner and hid behind the counter.

Alphonso crashed his tricycle into the door and grabbed the fox by the scruff of her neck.

'YOU CAN'T GET AWAY FROM ME!' he growled. 'You didn't give me my all-you-can-eat buffet, so NOW I'M GOING TO HAVE TO EAT YOU!'

'G-get away from you?' stammered Foxy. 'W-why on earth would I want to do that? I... err... just ran in here so I could... um... order your lunch. A-are you hungry?'

Alphonso eyed Foxy suspiciously.
Was this another trick? Still, he
was feeling rather peckish.
'Get me the biggest steak on
the menu!' he growled. Then he
squeezed his enormous belly in
behind a table and began to
sing:

'Food,
food,
food,

food, food,
food,
foodetty,
fooooood!'

Tony Ravioli smiled broadly and handed Foxy a pair of pink rubber gloves and an apron.

And, with that, Foxy DuBois, the smartest and most wily villain of them all, trudged into the back room. She filled the sink with steaming water, and began the long, lonely job of washing a tottering mountain of disgusting, dirty dishes.

KITCHEN ▶

The End

... Or is it?

Watch out for more Foxy Tales
coming soon to a bookshop
near you.

Alphonso's Ice Cream Sundae Recipe

Want to make a meal fit for an alligator? Here's how:

Ingredients

1 scoop strawberry ice cream

1 scoop chocolate ice cream

1 scoop vanilla ice cream

Large squirt of hot fudge sauce

Raspberries

Sprinkles

Cocktail umbrella

Cherry

Method

* Take one very large sundae glass.

* Place a handful of raspberries
  at the bottom.

* Layer ice cream till you have a
  lovely stripy design.

* Top with a large squirt of hot
  fudge sauce and sprinkles.

* Stick in a cocktail umbrella and
  pop a cherry on the top.

* Find a friendly alligator
  to eat it with you.

An Interview with a Fox

By

ANN RICE-PUDDING
THE DAILY BEAGLE

Ann: What is your full name?
Foxy: My pedigree name is:
Foxissima Ferrari Precious
Pumpkin O'Leary Bingtwistle
Bushy-tail DuBois the Third.

Ann: Gosh, that's a mouthful.
Foxy: Yes, it is rather wonderful
isn't it?

Ann: Err, yes. Right. So, Miss DuBois…

Foxy: Oh, call me Foxy, please.

Ann: All right. So, Foxy, can I ask you a personal question?

Foxy: Of course. I'll tell you anything you want to know – for a fee.

Ann: Have you ever been in love?

Foxy: I'm not answering THAT!

Ann: OK. What's your favourite colour?

Foxy: White. Definitely white. Or blue. Actually no. Pink. Pink is my favourite. And yellow.

Ann: If you had a million dollars, w̶ ̶ would you spend it on?

Foxy: Oh that's easy. Shoes. Lots and lots of shoes. I like shoes. And an alligator trap.

Ann: What has been your proudest moment so far?

Foxy: Winning the three-legged race at the village fête.

Ann: I heard you cheated in that race...

Foxy: So? I still WON didn't I!

Ann: What is your biggest regret?

Foxy: Meeting Alphonso and not having enough pairs of shoes.

Ann: And finally, Foxy, what advice do you have for other young foxes at the start of their careers?

Foxy: Never smile at an alligator.

Ann: Well, thank you, Miss DuBois, for taking the time to talk to me.

Foxy: It was my upmost and deepest pleasure. That'll be Five Hundred Dollars. Cash.

A Brief History of Egg Cups

By

MADAME VERONICA FOWL

It is with great pleasure that I introduce you to my famous and most esteemed egg-cup collection.

I have been collecting egg cups since I was three years old, when my great great great great grandmother gave me a

BOOOORR

very precious egg cup that her
great great great great great
grandmother had given her.
It is a plain white eggcup with no
patterns or marks or features at
all and has been shown several
times at the International Royal
Exhibition for Egg cups and other
Small Tableware in Cincinnati.

The first time it was shown
my great great g
grandmoth
prize, no les
you, was a g
honour for
household.

UNDER ALPHONSO'S BED EXCLUSIVE

Last week, after a long stake out, our reporters finally managed to gain access to Foxy DuBois' and Alphonso Alligator's apartment. They only broke one small window which they have promised to pay for. And now they bring you this exclusive report on the under bed world of Alphonso Alligator...

Seventeen crusty socks (all odd)

Six mouldy mugs

35 bits of bacon rind

Assorted sweet wrappers

Half chewed bones – various origins

A pair of glasses

Lipstick

TV remote control (broken)

Fluff

Several unidentified hairy things

Small tub of moustache wax

A copy of NIGHT TIME TALES FOR RESTLESS REPTILES

Food Magazine [with very dog—eared pages]

Foxy's left shoe that went missing last year

More fluff

Foxy's Top Trumps

Photocopy these pages then cut out the cards and stick them onto cardboard for extra strength.

Foxy

APPETITE - 4
GLAMOUR - 9
BRAINS - *10*
STRENGTH - 2
HIDDEN TALENT:
BIGGEST BUBBLE GUM BUBBLE - 6

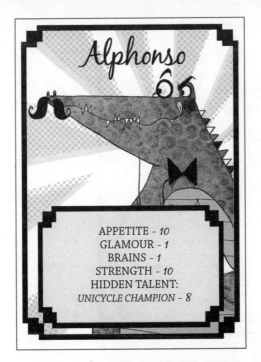

Alphonso

APPETITE - *10*
GLAMOUR - *1*
BRAINS - *1*
STRENGTH - *10*
HIDDEN TALENT:
UNICYCLE CHAMPION - 8

Little Norman

APPETITE - 2
GLAMOUR - 9
BRAINS - *8*
STRENGTH - *2*
HIDDEN TALENT:
*MOST BACK FLIPS WHILST
EATING DONUTS - 7*

Madame Fowl

APPETITE – *8*
GLAMOUR –*8*
BRAINS – 4
STRENGTH – 5
HIDDEN TALENT:
DON'T BE RIDICULOUS – 0

Tony Ravioli

APPETITE – *8*
GLAMOUR –*2*
BRAINS – 6
STRENGTH – 7
HIDDEN TALENT:
EXPERT BREAK DANCER – 10

Foxy's Favourite Books

A Shoppers' Guide to Shoes
by C. U. TREDWELL

Five Foxes on Treasure Island
by EDITH BRIGHTON

The Fox, the Witch and the Wardrobe
by C.S. LOONY

Fox in Socks
by DR SUITCASE

Goldilocks and the Three Foxes
by AVA LARFFE

Rearing Reptiles Safely
by MISS SING DIGIT

How to Write a Cunning Plan in 5 Easy Steps
by MAY B. MADD

Foxy's Family Tree

BENJAMIN
BUSHY-TAIL

LADY LILLY
BINGTWISTLE

CLOVER BANKSIDE
(PARENTAGE UNKNOWN)

SIR OSCAR BARNACLE
BINGTWISTLE BUSHY-TAIL

ZAZA DIAMONTE
BINGTWISTLE BUSHY-TAIL

LADY PETRONELLA
PRISSYPAWS BINGTWISTLE
BUSHY TAIL

*look how
important I am!*

FOXISSIMA FERRARI
BINGTWISTLE BUSHY

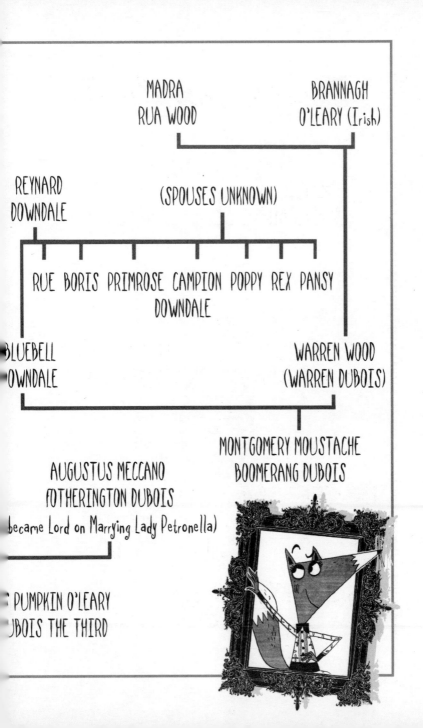

MADRA
RUA WOOD

BRANNAGH
O'LEARY (Irish)

REYNARD
DOWNDALE

(SPOUSES UNKNOWN)

RUE BORIS PRIMROSE CAMPION POPPY REX PANSY
DOWNDALE

BLUEBELL
DOWNDALE

WARREN WOOD
(WARREN DUBOIS)

MONTGOMERY MOUSTACHE
BOOMERANG DUBOIS

AUGUSTUS MECCANO
FOTHERINGTON DUBOIS
(became Lord on Marrying Lady Petronella)

PUMPKIN O'LEARY
DUBOIS THE THIRD

Alphonso's Family Tree